MONSTER CAN'T SLEEP

Virginia Mueller

pictures by Lynn Munsinger

Puffin Books

PUFFIN BOOKS
Published by the Penguin Group
Viking Penguin Inc., 40 West 23rd Street, New York, New York 10010, U.S.A.
Penguin Books Ltd, 27 Wrights Lane, London W8 5TZ England
Penguin Books Australia Ltd, Ringwood, Victoria, Australia
Penguin Books Canada Ltd, 2801 John Street, Markham, Ontario, Canada L3R 1B4
Penguin Books (N.Z.) Ltd, 182–190 Wairau Road, Auckland 10, New Zealand

Penguin Books Ltd, Registered Offices: Harmondsworth, Middlesex, England

First published in the United States of America by Albert Whitman & Company, 1986
Published in Puffin Books 1988
Text copyright © Virginia Mueller, 1986
Illustrations copyright © Lynn Munsinger, 1986
All rights reserved
Library of Congress Cataloging in Publication Data
Mueller, Virginia.
Monster can't sleep/by Virginia Mueller; pictures by Lynn Munsinger.
p. cm.
Summary: Monster can't fall asleep no matter what his parents try
until he tries to put his pet spider to sleep.
ISBN 0-14-050878-3
[1. Bedtime—Fiction. 2. Sleep—Fiction. 3. Monsters—Fiction.] I. Munsinger, Lynn, ill. II. Title.
PZ7.M879Mq 1988 [E]—dc 19 87-32870

Printed in Hong Kong by South China Printing Company

For Ann Fay. *V.M.*
For Doris Dahowski. *L.M.*

Monster was playing with his stuffed spider.

"It's bedtime," said Mother.

But Monster wasn't sleepy.

Father gave Monster some warm milk.

But Monster wasn't sleepy.

Mother read Monster a bedtime story.

But Monster wasn't sleepy.

Mother and Father kissed Monster good night.

But Monster wasn't sleepy.

"It's time for bed," said Mother. "Good night!"

"It's bedtime for Spider, too," said Monster.

He brought Spider some warm milk.

He told Spider a story.

He gave Spider a kiss.

"Good night, Spider," said Monster.

Then Monster went to sleep.